By James Gelsey

**SCHOLASTIC INC.**
**New York Toronto London Auckland Sydney**
**Mexico City New Delhi Hong Kong**

ISBN 0-439-23153-1



12 11 10 9 8 7 2 3 4 5/0

Cover and interior illustrations by Duendes del Sur
Cover and interior design by Madalina Stefan

Printed in the U.S.A.

First Scholastic printing, January 2001

You glance at your watch and see that you're late. You start running down the street, trying not to bump into anybody. You turn the corner and have to stop short.

A long line of people stretches down the street in front of you. You start walking down the street and then hear someone call your name. You look up and see Daphne waving at you from the front of the line.

"Hurry, we're next!" she shouts. You run the rest of the way down the street and meet up with Daphne, Fred, Velma, Shaggy, and Scooby-Doo.

"Next!" yells a voice from inside the door.

"Like, that's us!" Shaggy exclaims. "Let's go, Scooby-Doo!"

Scooby jumps up and runs inside with Shaggy before the rest of you take one step.

You follow Fred, Daphne, and Velma inside the restaurant and look around. It's not very big. There's a row of about ten round tables along the left side of the restaurant. Along the right side is a serving line. A waiter leads you and the gang to a table in the back.

Daphne turns around as she walks. "This place has the best soup," she says. "And there are no menus. They just keep bringing you different soups until you tell them to stop."

"Like, that's great, Daph," Shaggy says. "But what else do they have?"

"That's it, Shaggy," Daphne says. "Just soup."

"You mean people actually wait in line just to have soup?" Shaggy asks.

"Shaggy, people will wait in line for anything that's special," Velma says. "Like at the aquarium the other day."

"Man, don't bring that up," Shaggy moans. The waiter puts a bowl of soup in front of Scooby.

*"Rikes!"* he yells and dives under the table.

"What's the matter, Scooby?" Daphne asks.

Scooby's tail pops up. He changes it into an arrow and points at his bowl of soup.

"There's nothing in there but some Chinese cabbage," Velma says.

"That's not lettuce," Shaggy says. "That's seaweed! Make way, Scoob!" He dives under the table, too.

Fred, Daphne, and Velma all smile and shake their heads.

"They're just being silly," Daphne says. "Something in the soup reminds them of our last mystery."

"It was a real interesting one," Fred continues. "I'll bet you would have loved to helped us solve it."

"You still can, you know," Velma suggests. "Why don't you read our Clue Keeper and see if you can figure out the mystery, too?" She reaches into her pocket and takes out a small notebook. "Everything you need to know is in there," she says. "I should know because I took the notes this time."

"Remember, when you see  you've just met a suspect," Daphne says.

"And a  tells you that you've just found a clue," continues Fred. "After each

entry, we'll ask you some questions to help you along."

"So keep your own Clue Keeper and a pencil handy," Velma says. "And good luck solving *The Case of the Seaweed Monster.*"

# Clue Keeper Entry 1

We had just arrived at the Harbor View Aquarium to see the new dolphin show. We had to wait in the van for a few minutes for the rain to stop.

"Man, I can't believe Scoob and I had to miss the pizza eating contest at Luigi's just to go see some stupid dolphins," Shaggy complained.

"Actually, Shaggy, dolphins are believed to be the smartest mammals on the planet," I said.

*"Ruh-uh,"* Scooby disagreed.

"Scooby's right," Shaggy said. "Everyone knows that *people* are the smartest mammals. Right, Scoob?"

Scooby shook his head back and forth.

"Then who's smarter than dolphins and people?" I asked.

*"Rogs!"* shouted Scooby gleefully.

"Oh, brother!" Daphne exclaimed with a smile. "I can't wait to see this new dolphin show. They say the show features the statue of a golden dolphin that's just been brought up from the ocean floor."

"Like, I read about that in the newspaper," Shaggy said. "Isn't that statue supposed to have some kind of an ancient South Seas Island curse on it?"

"I read that, too," Daphne told Shaggy. "That just makes it even more interesting."

"Okay, everyone, it looks like the rain is letting up," Fred said. "Let's go in while we have the chance."

We got out of the van and ran across the parking lot to the aquarium entrance. There was a long line of people standing under the canopy just outside the building. Many of them were dressed in green ponchos. I knew the ponchos had been purchased at the aquarium gift store, because I had one myself that I'd bought the last time I was there. I sure wished I had it with me now.

As we got closer, we noticed a man in a green poncho. He smiled and chatted with all the damp people in line. When he saw us approach, he turned and smiled at us.

"Good afternoon," he said cheerily. "Welcome to the Harbor View Aquarium. I'm Jonah Bellows, the aquarium's director. I've just been telling folks about our great new dolphin show. You must see it."

"I don't know," Shaggy said. "Is that gold statue in the dolphin tank really cursed?"

Mr. Bellows scowled. "You read that in the newspaper, didn't you?" he said. "That article is killing my business. I think it's all part of a plot to shut down this aquarium!"

"Why would you think that?" Daphne asked. "Have other things been happening?"

Mr. Bellows looked around to see if anyone was listening. "Yes," he replied. "Very strange things."

"Zoinks!" cried Shaggy. "It's the Curse of the Golden Dolphin!"

"Shhhh!" Mr. Bellows shushed him. "Please don't say that so loud! It will frighten the other visitors."

The gang and I exchanged quick glances. I'm sure we were all thinking the same thing. Here was another mystery for us to solve.

A woman came up behind us in line. "Don't go in there!" she said so loudly that it was almost a shout. "Whatever you do. Don't enter that aquarium!"

We all turned around and faced her. She had long, straight black hair and dark eyes.

"Oh, not you again! Would you please keep your voice down?" Mr. Bellows said to her.

"I will not keep my voice down," the woman replied. "People have a right to know the truth!"

"The truth about what?" I asked.

"The truth about the way Jonah Bellows and his staff take advantage of dolphins for personal gain," the woman said.

"I don't understand," Daphne said.

"Allow me to explain," Mr. Bellows interjected before the woman could reply. "This is Carol Reef, from the Sea Creatures Defense Fund. She believes that we mistreat the dolphins that live in the aquarium."

"That's right," Carol said. "They train the dolphins to help find things out at sea. Things like sunken treasures and other valuables. Then Jonah and his people get

rich while all the dolphins get is a bucket of fish."

"I'm sure these young people would rather go inside than listen to us," Mr. Bellows said. He reached beneath his poncho and into his coat pocket. His hand came out holding some small cards.

"Here, take these," he said, handing us the cards. "These are VIP passes. Show them to the security guards and they'll take care of you. Enjoy your visit."

"Thanks, Mr. Bellows," Fred said, taking the cards. "Let's go, gang."

We continued on our way to the front doors. Jonah Bellows and Carol Reef started arguing again. We heard Carol say one last thing to Mr. Bellows.

"I don't care what you say, you're going to stop what you're doing!" she shouted. "Even if it means I have to find some way to close this whole aquarium down all by myself!"

# Velma's Mystery-Solving Tips

"Jinkies, she sure was angry, wasn't she? There's no way you could have missed the in this entry. So open up your Clue Keeper, grab a pen or pencil, and start your entry for the first suspect by answering these questions."

1. What is the suspect's name?

2. What is she doing at the aquarium?

3. Why do you think she is so angry at Jonah Bellows?

"Once you're done taking your own notes, read on!"

## Clue Keeper Entry 2

We walked into the aquarium and showed the passes to the security guard. He nodded his head and pointed to a silver door next to the information booth.

"Right through there, folks," he said. "If anyone asks, show them the passes. Just stay away from the restricted areas."

"Like, how will we know which are the restricted areas?" Shaggy asked.

"You'll see big signs that say, 'restricted area,'" the guard replied with a smile. "Enjoy your visit."

"Thanks," I said. "Let's go, gang."

We opened the silver door and walked into a brightly lit corridor. There was a long staircase leading down to another door. We walked through that door.

"Jinkies!" I exclaimed as I looked around. "This is amazing!"

The wall in front of us looked like it was made of glass. We could see right through it into a huge tank of water.

"Man, that's the largest indoor swimming pool I've ever seen!" Shaggy added.

"Shaggy, that's not a swimming pool," Daphne said. "That's the dolphin tank behind that glass!"

We all looked up and saw three dolphins swimming right toward us.

"Actually, it's a special kind of see-through plastic called plexiglass," we heard

Jonah Bellows say. He walked over to us. "It's several inches thick, so you don't have to worry about any dolphins — or water — getting out."

Scooby crept up to the tank. He got closer and closer until his nose and front paws were pressed against the plexiglass. A dolphin suddenly swam up and pressed his nose against the inside of the tank.

*"Rikes!"* Scooby yelled as he jumped back.

"Relax, Scooby," I said. "He's only play-

ing. More proof that dolphins really are smarter than dogs."

"What happened to Carol Reef?" Daphne asked.

"I got tired of being yelled at so I came back inside," Mr. Bellows replied. "I'm sure I haven't heard the last of her."

"Mr. Bellows, is that someone in the tank with the dolphins?" I asked.

We all got closer to get a better look. We could see a figure in the water.

"That's Gil Gupperman," Jonah said. "He's my assistant. Right now, he's putting the finishing touches on our newest display."

We watched as the figure made a sudden gesture with his arms. He spun around as one of the dolphins swam past him. The figure waved his arms and tried to grab one of the dolphins. Then he gave up and swam over to one side of the tank. A moment later, we heard a hissing sound.

"That's the air lock," Mr. Bellows explained. "There's a small chamber that connects the tank with this room. When

Gil goes in, he closes the door. The water is pumped out and air is pumped in. When the outer door opens, it makes the hissing sound."

Gil Gupperman stepped out of the air lock.

"That's it, I've had it!" he yelled at Mr. Bellows. "Those dolphins are out to get me!"

"They're not out to get you, Gil," Mr. Bellows said calmly. "They're just playing."

"I don't care what they're doing," Gil complained. "They treat me as badly as you do. I've been working here eight years. It's bad enough I'm still cleaning fish tanks and doing underwater maintenance. Now I have to be teased by dolphins. I don't care how much treasure those overgrown guppies found, I'm not going to take it anymore!"

"Uh, Gil, let's not get excited now," Mr. Bellows tried to calm him. "Why don't you and I have a little talk in private?"

"No more talks!" Gil ordered. "I want things to change around here or there'll be trouble. And lots of it!" Gil took a white card out of his pocket. He slid it through a black box beside a door with a "restricted" sign on it. We heard a clicking sound. Gil opened the door, went inside, and slammed the door shut behind him.

"When he mentioned treasure, was he referring to the golden dolphin?" Fred asked.

"Well, kids, I guess I have some explaining to do," Jonah said with a sigh.

## Daphne's Mystery-Solving Tips

"That was quite a moment, wasn't it? Did you catch the 👀? Great. Open up your Clue Keeper and answer these questions."

1. What is the suspect's name?

2. What does he do at the aquarium?

3. Why do you think he's so angry at Jonah Bellows?

"Once you've jotted down your notes, read on to find out what Jonah Bellows had to say."

# Clue Keeper Entry 3

Jonah Bellows pointed to the dolphin tank.

"If you look closely, you can see something in the middle of the tank," he said.

We all got close to the plexiglass and looked inside.

"I think I see something," Daphne said.

"No, that's just a dolphin," I said.

"You're both right," Mr. Bellows remarked. "It's a dolphin, but it's made out of solid gold."

"The Golden Dolphin?" Shaggy asked. "As in fourteen karats?"

"Eighteen, actually," a voice said from behind us.

We all turned around and saw a tall man wearing a white lab coat. He had very thick, round eyeglasses.

"Ah, Dr. Piedmont," Mr. Bellows said. "Dr. Piedmont is our visiting dolphin expert."

Dr. Piedmont frowned when he heard this.

"Please, Jonah, I am more than a dolphin expert," he said. "You are forgetting that I am the one who found the Golden Dolphin."

"No, the dolphins found the Golden Dolphin," Mr. Bellows corrected.

"Because I trained the dolphins to hunt for treasure," Dr. Piedmont continued. "And I also had the map of where to look."

"Yes, but the aquarium funded the expedition," Mr. Bellows countered. "You are just a short-term, temporary employee of the aquarium. You've only been here a matter of months."

"The most important few months in the history of this aquarium!" Dr. Piedmont shouted.

We could tell that Jonah Bellows and Dr. Piedmont were about to get into an ugly fight.

"Excuse me, Dr. Piedmont," I interrupted. "Is it true that dolphins are the smartest mammals?"

"Of course, young lady," Dr. Piedmont replied. "That is why I work with them. And that is why they were able to find the treasure. And that is why I deserve a bigger reward for my efforts."

"So, that is what this is about?" Mr. Bellows asked. "You want to share in the profits from the Golden Dolphin? Let me tell you something, Dr. Piedmont. The Golden Dolphin will not be sold. It will remain a permanent part of the aquarium's exhibit. And if you don't like it, I suggest you think about finding work some place else!"

Jonah Bellows abruptly left.

"He doesn't know with whom he is dealing," Dr. Piedmont grumbled.

"Excuse me for asking," Daphne said quietly. "But what's so special about the Golden Dolphin?"

"Aside from the fact that it's made of gold?" Fred added.

"Legend has it that it is over three hundred years old," Dr. Piedmont explained. "A tribe of South Sea natives thought it brought them luck. But then a band of pirates stole it from the natives. At first, the pirates planned to sell it, but, later they actually tossed it off their pirate ship when they discovered the curse."

Shaggy and Scooby suddenly turned around.

"Like, d-d-did you say c-c-curse?" Shaggy asked nervously. "You mean . . . it's true?"

"Yes, the curse is very real," Dr. Piedmont continued. "The natives put a curse on the statue so that whoever has it will be haunted by a mysterious sea creature. But I don't believe in curses. I only believe in being fairly rewarded for one's work. Mark my words, I'll see to it that Jonah Bellows gives me my due, or else! Now if you'll excuse me, I have some work to do."

Dr. Piedmont walked away from us. He

took a card from his pocket and swiped it through the electronic lock.

"Ladies and gentlemen," came a voice from a loudspeaker. "The dolphin show will start in five minutes."

"Well, gang," Fred said. "Let's get out of here and go watch the show."

"And maybe we can stop at the snack bar along the way," Shaggy said. "Swimming always makes me hungry."

“But you haven’t been swimming,” Daphne said.

“I know, but those dolphins have,” Shaggy replied. “Just watching them is enough to work up an appetite!”

# Fred's Mystery-Solving Tips

"I'll bet you saw the 👀 in this entry, right? Great. So look over these questions and write down the answers in your Clue Keeper."

1. What is the suspect's name?

2. What is his connection to the aquarium?

3. Why is he so angry at Jonah Bellows?

"Once you're done, read on to find out what happened next."

# Clue Keeper Entry 4

We left the tank area the way we came in. Once we were back in the aquarium lobby, we followed the signs to the dolphin show. We walked through an archway and into an outdoor theater. We showed our passes to one of the aquarium employees. He led us to special seats right up front and handed us five small green packages.

*"Runch!"* Scooby shouted happily. He ripped open the package and unfolded a big green poncho.

"Ruh?" Scooby said.

"That's a poncho, Scooby," I said. "You're supposed to put it on just in case we get splashed during the show."

We all put on our ponchos and looked around.

"Wow!" Daphne exclaimed. "The dolphin tank looks even bigger from up here."

And it was. Downstairs, we only saw part of the bottom of the tank. But when we were sitting in the theater, we saw the whole top of the tank. It must have been as big as a football field. And there was a big dock on the other side of the tank where the dolphin trainers stood.

"Ladies and gentlemen, welcome to Dolphin World at the Harbor View Aquarium!" boomed a voice from the loudspeaker. "Please welcome the royal dolphin family!" The three dolphins in the tank jumped out of the water and tumbled through the air be-

fore splashing back down. Some of the water splashed us.

"Now aren't you glad you didn't eat your poncho?" Daphne asked Scooby with a smile.

The show continued for several minutes. The voice over the loudspeaker introduced the various tricks. The trainers made gestures with their arms and hands. Then the dolphins jumped through hoops, played basketball, or did other kinds of flips, leaps, and fancy tricks.

"And now, please welcome the latest addition to the royal family," the voice announced. "It was freed from its resting place on the bottom of the ocean by its real-life cousins. Ladies and gentlemen, please welcome the Golden Dolphin."

A huge fountain of water sprayed up in the center of the dolphin tank. The three dolphins swam around and around in a big circle. Slowly, something started rising out of the water. It was hard to see with all the splashing and spraying, but it looked like the Golden Dolphin.

"Hey, there's something on the Golden Dolphin," Fred said.

"It looks like a really big clump of seaweed to me," I said.

"Man, like they couldn't even clean off the statue before they showed it to everyone?" Shaggy asked.

Then the seaweed started to move.

Everyone in the audience gasped.

The seaweed slowly stood up until it was standing on top of the Golden Dolphin. Now it looked more like some kind of creature than just a pile of seaweed.

The creature slowly looked around and then let out a mighty roar.

"Aaaaaaahhhhhhhhrrrrrrrr!" it bellowed, its voice filling the amphitheater. "Free the Golden Dolphin, or else!!!" it shouted in a creaky, scary voice.

"Zoinks!" Shaggy exclaimed. "Like, the seaweed's talking! The curse has come true. Let's get out of here, Scooby!"

*"Right!"* Scooby agreed. He and Shaggy stood up to run away, but it was too late. Everyone else in the amphitheater also had that idea. As the people rushed out yelling, Jonah Bellows ran out onto the dock.

"Wait! Wait!" he shouted. "It's all part of the show! Come back, please!" But it was too

late. Everyone was gone. And when we looked back at the Golden Dolphin, so was the seaweed monster.

Fred, Daphne, and I looked at each other and shook our heads. Mr. Bellows was lying. His panicked expression told us that much. This wasn't part of the show at all.

"Hey, Mr. Bellows!" Fred called. "Don't worry about a thing. Mystery, Inc. is on the case!"

## Clue Keeper Entry 5

The first thing we wanted to do was get a closer look at the Golden Dolphin itself. We left our seats and followed the walkway around to the other side of the dolphin tank. Jonah Bellows was still standing there, looking around.

"I can't believe it," he sighed. "It was bad

enough that people heard about the curse on the Golden Dolphin. Once word gets out about this seaweed monster, I'll be ruined. No one's going to visit an aquarium with a cursed statue and a monster."

"And, like, that includes us," Shaggy said. "Let's go, Scooby-Doo. We're outta here."

"Oh, no you don't," I said to them. "We're going to need your help finding clues. It's the least we can do to repay Mr. Bellows for the free passes he gave us."

"If it's all right with you, Mr. Bellows," Fred said. "We'd like to look around."

"Sure, why not?" Mr. Bellows said. "I can use all the help I can get."

"Great!" Fred said. "Daphne and I will look around up here to see if there's any sign of the monster."

"Shaggy, Scooby, and I will go back downstairs," I said. "If that seaweed monster came up with the statue, we'll be able to see any clues in the tank through the plexiglass."

"Good idea, Velma," Daphne said. "Let's all meet back here as soon as we can."

"Let's go, boys," I said to Shaggy and Scooby.

"Like, do you think we can stop at the snack bar on the way down," Shaggy said as we left the amphitheater. "We never did quite make it there before the dolphin show."

"We'll see about that later," I said. "Right now we have more important things to do."

"More important than eating?!" Shaggy exclaimed. "Like, in my book, there's no such thing."

"That's because your book is a cookbook," I replied. We walked down the short flight of stairs and opened the metal door.

"I'm going to see if there's anything suspicious in the tank," I continued. "You two see if anything catches your eye out here."

I walked over to the tank and peered through the thick plexiglass. I could see the dolphins swimming around. I could also see the elevated platform holding the Golden Dolphin. But there was no sign of anything else.

"Did you two find anything yet?" I asked

Shaggy and Scooby as I turned around. But instead of looking for clues, Shaggy and Scooby were gone.

"I'll bet they went to the snack bar after all." I sighed. Then I heard a sound coming from the end of the hall. It was some kind of thumping. As I walked down the hall, the thumping grew louder. Then I heard some muffled voices.

I reached the end of the hall and stood in front of a door. The thumping and voices were coming from behind it.

"Oh, no," I groaned. "Shaggy and Scooby are in the air lock."

There were no handles on the door, so I couldn't just open it. I noticed one of the security card locks mounted on the wall next to the door. Without a card, I couldn't open the door.

*But I'll bet there's some kind of emergency release,* I thought to myself. I looked a little more closely and found a hidden red emergency button. I pushed it and heard a hiss and a click, and then the door opened. Shaggy and Scooby came tumbling out.

"Boy, are we glad to see you, Velma," Shaggy gasped.

"What happened?" I asked.

"Scooby and I were looking for clues. We thought we saw something in there. So we stepped inside, and then the door closed behind us. Man, that was really freaky."

Just then, something green on the floor caught my eye. I picked it up and looked at it carefully.

"Like, that's what we saw," Shaggy said.

*"Rat ris rit?"* asked Scooby.

"I'm not sure, Scooby," I answered. "It looks like seaweed, but it feels like plastic. I wonder if it's a piece of something. If you ask me, I think we've found our first clue. Let's go tell Fred and Daphne."

# Shaggy and Scooby's Mystery-Solving Tips

"Like, did you catch the in that last entry? Yeah, it wasn't too hard to miss. So grab your Clue Keeper and answer these questions about it."

1. What is the clue you just found?

2. What do you think this clue has to do with the sea-weed monster?

3. Who else do you remember wearing something that looks and feels like that?

## Clue Keeper Entry 6

Fred, Daphne, and Mr. Bellows were standing on the dock at the far end of the big, outdoor dolphin tank. They were looking at something in Fred's hand. Daphne looked up, saw us, and waved at us to hurry up. When we got there, Fred showed us what he was holding.

"So, like, you found a credit card," Shaggy said. "What's the big deal?"

"This is not a credit card, Shaggy," Daphne said. "It's a security card. And the big deal is what this security card unlocks."

"Daphne's right," Fred added. "We found it on the ground next to the tank. The seaweed monster must've lost it by accident."

"But we didn't see the seaweed monster come out of the tank," I said. "How could it drop anything out here?"

"We think he dropped it while he was in the tank," Daphne explained. "And it got sprayed out by the fountain of water when the Golden Dolphin came up."

"Of course!" I exclaimed. "That makes perfect sense."

"Man, Scoob and I can't take the suspense anymore," Shaggy blurted out. "What does the card unlock?"

"The lab room downstairs," Mr. Bellows replied. "And the air lock."

"Hmm, interesting," I said. "Now take a look at this."

I showed Fred, Daphne, and Mr. Bellows

the piece of green plastic material Shaggy found in the air lock.

"Why, this looks like it came from one of the aquarium ponchos," Mr. Bellows said.

"Now imagine a whole costume made up of these little pieces of green poncho," I said. "Now what do you get?"

"Zoinks! The seaweed monster!" Shaggy exclaimed.

"Very good, Shaggy," I said. "How did you guess?"

"I didn't!" Shaggy replied in a shaky voice. "It's the seaweed monster! For real!"

We all whirled around and saw the seaweed monster running right toward us!

"Quick, everyone, let's get out of here!" Fred called.

"Follow me!" Mr. Bellows called as he ran toward the seats on the other side of the dolphin tank. We followed him down a narrow passageway under the seats. There were a lot of stairs. We went through a door, and the next thing we knew, we were back downstairs by the dolphin tank.

"Man, does every staircase in this place lead back here?" Shaggy asked.

"Only the ones around the amphitheater," Mr. Bellows replied. "But they're all pretty much hidden and off limits to regular visitors."

"If there's more than one staircase," Daphne said, "that means the seaweed monster must have used one of the others to scare us."

"Things are starting to make sense now," I said. "I have a hunch that our seaweed monster is about to be all washed up."

"Velma's right," Fred agreed. "Gang, it's time to set a trap."

# Daphne's Mystery-Solving Tips

"Wow, so much happened in this entry! Did you find both Great! Now open up your Clue Keeper and answer these questions about the clues you found."

1. What clues did you find?

2. What do they have to do with the seaweed monster?

3. Which of the suspects would most likely have access to the clues on a regular basis?

"I know it's a lot of stuff to think about, but I know you can handle it! Now read the next entry to see how we caught the seaweed monster."

## Clue Keeper Entry 7

We decided that the best way to lure the seaweed monster back was to continue with the dolphin show. Once the Golden Dolphin made its appearance, the monster was sure to come back and try to scare us again. Mr. Bellows said he'd help us and went to get the dolphins ready.

"Like, sounds like a good plan," Shaggy said. "But what's the catch?"

"There's no catch," Daphne said.

"Oh, yes there is," Shaggy said shaking his head. "There's always a catch. And it usually involves me and Scooby."

"Well, Shaggy . . ." Fred began.

"Here we go," Shaggy moaned.

"I'll need your help on the far side of the tank," Fred said. "That way, when the seaweed monster runs by, we can use the big nets over there to catch him."

*"Rand ree?"* Scooby asked.

"Scooby, you have the easiest job," I said. "All you have to do is take a short run."

*"Ruh?"* Scooby asked, sitting up.

"That's not such a big deal for a brave dog like you, right Scooby?" Daphne said to him.

*"Ruh-uh,"* Scooby disagreed. He crossed his paws.

"I know what will make him even braver," I said. "How about a Scooby Snack?"

Scooby licked his lips.

*"Rokay!"* he agreed.

I tossed a Scooby Snack into the air and he gobbled it down.

Mr. Bellows came back over to the rest of us.

"Everything's ready," he said. "I'll be over here to handle the dolphins."

"Great," Fred said. "Shaggy and I will hide at the other end with those big nets. Scooby, you wait with Mr. Bellows. When the seaweed monster appears, get him to chase you down to us."

*"Right!"* Scooby replied, saluting Fred like a soldier.

"Daphne and I will sit in the VIP box and cheer," I said. "That way, the seaweed monster will think there's a real show going on."

We all took our places. The voice over the loudspeaker came back on to narrate the show. Mr. Bellows raised his arms above his head and the dolphins suddenly jumped out of the water. They each turned a double flip and splashed back into the tank. Soon, the water started bubbling and fountains of water sprayed up into the air. The Golden Dolphin slowly rose to the surface. Daphne and I cheered and applauded.

Suddenly, we heard a noise come from under our seats. The seaweed monster ran out from one of the secret passages beneath the stands. It raised its seaweedy arms and let out a terrible howl.

*"Rikes!"* Scooby shouted. Scooby started to run and the seaweed monster started to chase him.

As Scooby ran, his paws slipped on the puddles left over from the big dolphin splashes. He slid along the ground right past where Fred and Shaggy were hiding. The seaweed monster also lost his footing.

Fred and Shaggy threw the net down but the seaweed monster was sliding too fast.

*"Ruh-oh!"* Scooby gasped. He and the seaweed monster slid off the dock and onto a short diving board extending over the dolphin tank.

SPLASH!

Scooby started dog paddling as hard as he could. The seaweed monster swam after him. Just as the seaweed monster was about to grab Scooby's tail, the monster suddenly shot into the air.

It splashed back into the tank and then went up again. Two of the dolphins were tossing the monster around like a beach ball! The other dolphin swam under Scooby and took him back to the side of the tank. Fred and Shaggy helped him out.

*"Ranks!"* Scooby thanked the dolphin.

As Daphne and I ran over, we saw one of the dolphins flip the seaweed monster high into the air. The monster sailed through the air and landed right in the dolphin netting at the far end of the tank.

“Man, talk about a perfect catch,” Shaggy said.

We all ran over to the netting.

“Now let’s see who’s really behind all this,” Fred said.

"That was some adventure, wasn't it?" says Daphne. "And now that you've finished reading the Clue Keeper, I'll bet you're ready to solve the mystery."

"Open up your own Clue Keeper and take a look at your notes," Fred suggests. "Review your list of suspects to refresh your memory."

"Then look at your clues," Velma continues. "Try to figure out which of the suspects go with each of the clues. I'm sure things will come together pretty quickly."

"Once you've figured it out for yourself, we'll give you the real solution to the mystery," Daphne says.

"It was Gil Gupperman," Velma says. "And I have a hunch you guessed that, too."

"All of the suspects had reasons for wanting to scare people away from the aquarium," Fred reminds you. "And they all seemed to want to get revenge on Jonah Bellows. That's why the clues were so important."

"Remember the first clue?" Daphne asks.

"That piece of green plastic was cut from one of the green aquarium ponchos. In fact, the seaweed monster's whole costume was made from a bunch of ponchos."

"But any one of the suspects could have done that," Fred says. "Even Carol Reef could have bought the ponchos at the gift shop."

"And since both Dr. Piedmont and Gil Gupperman worked at the aquarium," Velma adds, "they would be able to get their hands on them at any time."

"The second clue we found was the security pass card," Daphne says. "And only an aquarium employee would have one of those. That eliminated Carol Reef."

"But still kept suspicion on Dr. Piedmont and Gil," Fred says. "It wasn't until the last clue that everything fell into place."

"The last clue was knowing about the secret staircases down to the underground rooms. And only a full-time aquarium employee would know about those," Daphne says.

"Dr. Piedmont was only a visitor to the aquarium, remember?" Fred asks. "That left only Gil Gupperman."

"It looks like you solved another exciting mystery," Velma says.

"Excuse me," Shaggy says. "But there's still one mystery left to solve."

"What's that?" asks Daphne.

"Like, the mystery of how to convince the cooks here to make Scooby and me some pizza soup!"

Everyone starts laughing.

*"Rooby-rooby-roo!"* Scooby barks happily.